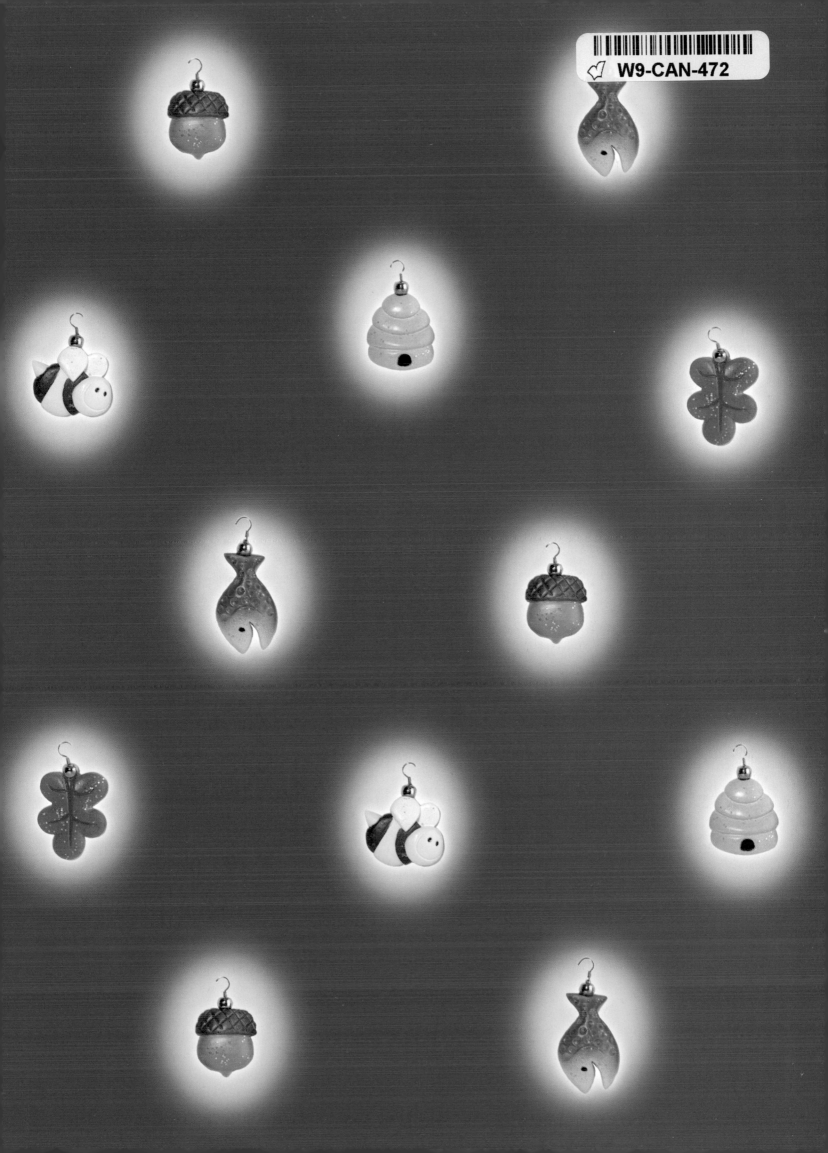

THE TEDDY BEARS'

Night Before Christmas

The Kissenbear Family

To my parents,
Mary and Michael,
for their unflagging support
and encouragement.
With love,
MS

Special thanks to: My assistants, Giovanni Di Mola and Kristen Sard; Nat Baines for his craftiness; my agent, Olive Head; Matthew Reinhardt for the quirky toys and props; Bruce Morozko for the sets; Todd Moore and Lisa Sacco for styling and inspiration; Linda Spiegel for her endless creativity in constructing the bears and reindeer; Paula Lettiere for costume design, organization, and other assorted talents; Vicki Khuzami for painted backdrops; and Carol Huntakul for sewing skills. This project would have been impossible without the generosity of these wonderful people.

Heartfelt thanks to my editor, Diane Muldrow, for her vision and faith to begin this book with me; to Bernette Ford and Jean Feiwel for truly getting it off the ground; and to Patti Ann Harris and Edie Weinberg for their ever-encouraging and enthusiastic suggestions.
—MS

Library of Congress Catalog Card Number: 98-61147

ISBN 0-590-03243-7

10 9 8 7 6 5 4 3 2 1   9/9 0/0 01 02 03 04

Printed in Singapore   46
First printing, September 1999

THE TEDDY BEARS'
Night Before Christmas

by Clement Clarke Moore

Photo illustration by Monica Stevenson

Cartwheel BOOKS®

SCHOLASTIC INC.

New York Toronto London Auckland Sydney Mexico City New Delhi Hong Kong

'Twas the night before Christmas,
when all through the house
Not a creature was stirring,
not even a mouse.

The stockings were hung
by the chimney with care,
In hopes that St. Nicholas
soon would be there.

The children were nestled all snug in their beds,

While visions of sugarplums danced in their heads.

And Mamma in her kerchief,
   and I in my cap,
Had just settled down
   for a long winter's nap,

When out on the lawn
   there arose such a clatter,
I sprang from the bed
   to see what was the matter.

Away to the window
   I flew like a flash,
Tore open the shutters
   and threw up the sash.

The moon on the breast
   of the new-fallen snow,
Gave the luster of midday
   to objects below.

When, what to my wondering
    eyes should appear,
But a miniature sleigh
    and eight tiny reindeer.

With a little old driver,
    so lively and quick,
I knew in a moment
    it must be St. Nick.

More rapid than eagles
his coursers they came,
And he whistled, and shouted,
and called them by name:

"Now, Dasher! Now, Dancer!

Now, Prancer and Vixen!

On, Comet! On, Cupid!

On, Donder and Blitzen!

To the top of the porch!
To the top of the wall!
Now dash away! Dash away!
Dash away all!"

As dry leaves that before
    the wild hurricane fly,
When they meet with an obstacle,
    mount to the sky,

So up to the housetop
    the coursers they flew,
With the sleigh full of toys,
    and St. Nicholas, too.

And then in a twinkling,
    I heard on the roof,
The prancing and pawing
    of each little hoof—

As I drew in my head,
    and was turning around,
Down the chimney St. Nicholas
    came with a bound.

He was dressed all in fur,
    from his head to his foot,
And his clothes were all tarnished
    with ashes and soot.

A bundle of toys,
    he had flung on his back,
And he looked like a peddler
    just opening his pack.

His eyes—how they twinkled!
　　His dimples, how merry!
His cheeks were like roses,
　　his nose like a cherry!

His droll little mouth
　　was drawn up like a bow,
And the beard of his chin
　　was as white as the snow.

The stump of his pipe
　　he held tight in his teeth,
And the smoke it encircled
　　his head like a wreath.

He had a broad face
    and a little round belly,
That shook when he laughed,
    like a bowlful of jelly.

He was chubby and plump,
    a right jolly old elf,
And I laughed when I saw him,
    in spite of myself.

A wink of his eye
      and a twist of his head,
Soon gave me to know
      I had nothing to dread.

He spoke not a word,
      but went straight to his work,
And filled all the stockings,
      then turned with a jerk.

And laying his finger
    aside of his nose,
And giving a nod,
    up the chimney he rose.

He sprang to his sleigh,
to his team gave a whistle,
And away they all flew
like the down of a thistle.

But I heard him exclaim,
as he drove out of sight,

And to all a good night."

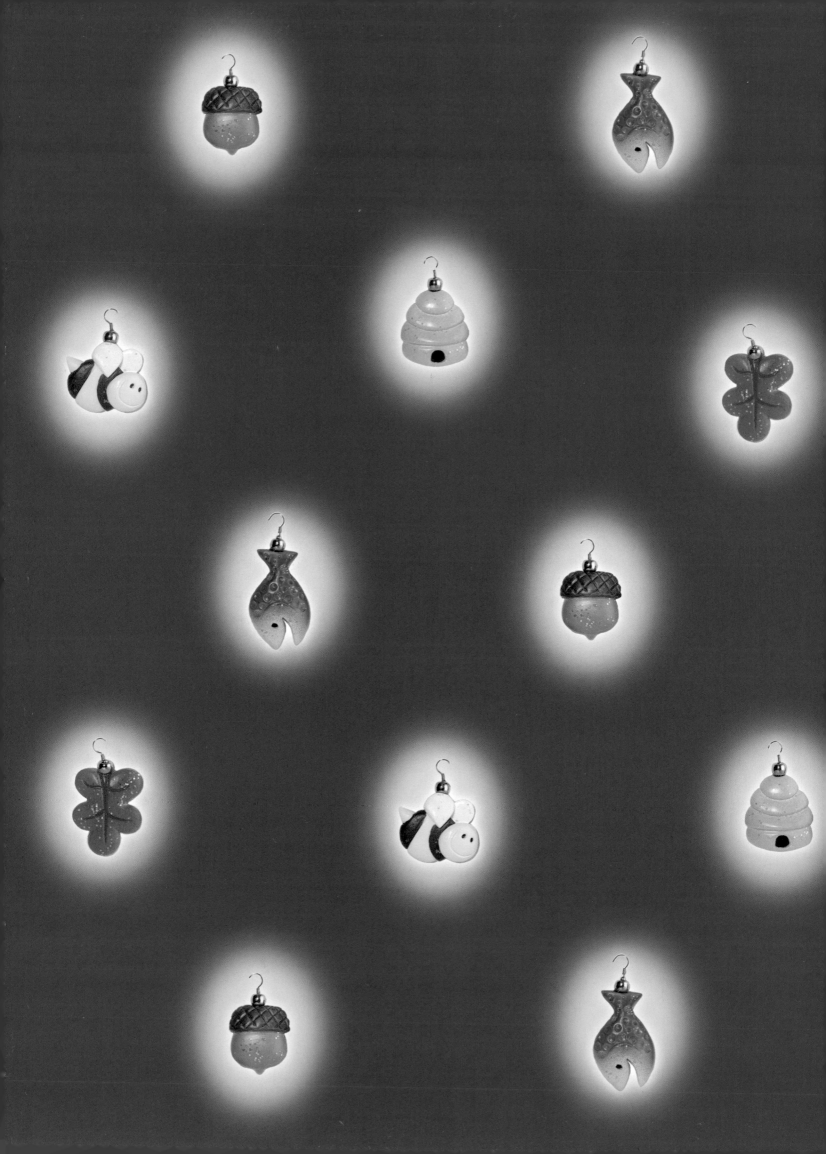